LOTTIE LOSTALOT:
A MAGICAL ADVENTURE

Author

PJ SANDZ

Illustrations

WE.ARE.ALIEN

Grosvenor House
Publishing Limited

This book is published by
Grosvenor House Publishing Ltd
Link House
140 The Broadway, Tolworth, Surrey, KT6 7HT.
www.grosvenorhousepublishing.co.uk

This book is a work of fiction. Any resemblance to
people or events, past or present, is purely coincidental.

A CIP record for this book
is available from the British Library

ISBN 978-1-80381-507-7
eBook ISBN 978-1-80381-508-4

*My amazing daughter, Katy,
is the inspiration behind the
story of Lottie Lostalot.*

*Growing up, she was always getting lost:
at home, at school, out shopping. Then,
in her mid twenties, she was diagnosed
with autism, and everything became clear.
Each of our lives have now changed,
in a positive way, and we have acquired
Jack, an autism assistance dog,
and a new vacuum!*

*I hope you enjoy reading this
magical adventure as much as
I enjoyed writing it.*

INTRODUCTION

Lottie is a little girl who
is always getting lost.

Because of this, her family
call her Lottie Lostalot.

When they go on holiday, Lottie,
of course, gets lost, and this is the
start of an amazing, magical adventure!

CHAPTERS

CHAPTER ONE

LOTTIE LOSTALOT

Lottie Lostalot lived with her rather eccentric family in a large and quirky cottage her father had built. It was not far from the little village of Hollands Down, in the perfect spot: halfway up a hill, and close to a wood that seemed to go on forever. There were Mother, Father, and Lottie's two older brothers, Freddy and Ben. The cottage had taken rather a long time to finish, and there were still some bits that Mother wasn't completely happy with, but the family loved it there, and thought that Father was very clever! The two boys were always exploring in the wood, but would never take their little sister with them, in case she got lost!

Lottie Lostalot wasn't her real name, but she was *always* getting lost, so this is what her family affectionately called her!

"I don't know what to do with you, Lottie," her mother would say. "I just can't understand how you manage to get lost all the time!"

"I don't understand either, Mother," Lottie would reply. "I try *so* hard, but it doesn't seem to help!"

When Lottie was very little, she got lost when shopping with her mother. However, she didn't know she was lost. It was only when Mother came rushing up, out of breath, with tears on her cheek, shouting, "Lottie! Lottie! Thank goodness I've found you. I turned around for a second, and you'd vanished! How many times have I told you not to wander off?" that Lottie realised she *must* have been lost!

Still, she didn't know what all the fuss was about. "I just wanted to play on the wooden dragon, Mother," she said.

"Goodness," said Mother. "You *did* give me a fright! You mustn't leave my side when we are out shopping."

Lottie looked very crestfallen. The shop had a large wooden dragon that you could climb on and slide down, and all the children loved playing on it. "I'm sorry, Mother," she whispered, secretly thinking that Mother was making a fuss about nothing. She wasn't lost; she knew exactly where she was. Shopping was boring. Playing on the dragon was much more fun!

When the time came to go to school, Lottie was very excited. She was going to learn new things and make new friends, and perhaps she wouldn't be in trouble with Mother so much. She did try very hard to do her best, but somehow, things always seemed to go wrong. Poor Mother could regularly be heard shouting, "Lottie! Lottie! Where are you? Has anyone seen Lottie? I can't find her anywhere!"

Lottie very much hoped that things would improve when she was at school, but instead of Mother trying to find her, it was the teachers! "Has anyone seen Lottie?" they would ask the other children when she was late for class, and when, eventually, she would appear, they would say, "Lottie, where have you been? You are late for class!" to which Lottie would reply, "I'm very sorry, Miss. I got lost!"

It happened so often, that after a while, everybody expected Lottie to be late for class, and she stopped getting told off.

Eventually, school finished for summer, and all the children were very excited. "Holidays, holidays!" they shouted, chattering nineteen to the dozen about going to the seaside with their parents, or to faraway places on an aeroplane.

Lottie ran home as fast as her legs would take her. "Mother, Mother, are we going on our holidays?" she cried.

"Of course we are," said Mother. "We are all going camping on a little farm not far from a lovely, sandy beach. It's a magical place, Lottie, and you and your brothers will love it there, but you must promise me you won't get lost!"

"I promise, Mother! I will do my very best not to get lost. I really don't know how it happens at all."

So Lottie, Freddy, and Ben, helped Mother and Father pack the car. In went a large tent, buckets and spades, and all the paraphernalia needed for a splendid holiday.

CHAPTER TWO

A MAGICAL PLACE

It was quite a long journey to the
campsite, and Lottie was very
fidgety and bored. "Are we there yet?" she kept
asking.

"Not yet," Mother would reply. "Have patience,
Lottie. It is a virtue, after all!"

"What's a virtue?" Lottie asked.

"Oh *do* shut up!" Freddy said. "Just sit quietly till
we get there."

With a huff and a puff, Lottie crossed her arms
and legs, and glared out the window.

Eventually, the car slowed down, and turned in
through the gates of a big farmyard.

Lottie sat up straight and pressed her nose
against the window. "We're here, we're here!"

she cried excitedly. "Stop the car, I want to get out!"

Father switched the engine off and put the handbrake on. "Righty oh," he said. "Everyone stay in the car while I get out and ask where we can put our tent."

A rather scruffy old lady in large wellington boots, followed by an equally scruffy, clucking chicken appeared at the door of the farmhouse. "Can I help you?" she asked.

"I hope so," said Father. "We are on our holidays and would like to camp here for a few days."

"Well, well, well," said the old lady, peering into the car and seeing Lottie's nose squished up against the glass. "We are quite busy, but I'm sure we can find a space for you," she said, giving Lottie a big wink!

Lottie clapped her hands and jumped up and down in her seat, making the car rock from side to side, and digging an elbow into Freddy's ribs in the process.

"Lottie!" the boys shouted. "*Do* sit still!"

"Thank you," said Father. "That's brilliant! Right everyone, lets go and find a spot to camp." And with that, he clambered back in the car, and drove slowly through the farmyard, scattering chickens in all directions, amid lots of squawking and clucking.

The car bounced across the field, until Father said, "Here will do, I think! Come on, boys, let's get the tent up before it gets dark. And Lottie, don't wander away. I don't want you getting lost!"

So the whole family busied themselves (even Lottie was helpful, carrying the tent pegs) and as the moon started to rise in the sky, they were all ready to settle down for a good night's sleep.

The next morning, they were all woken by a very loud "Cock-a-doodle-doo," from the old cockerel in the farmyard, and the sounds of swallows, swooping and twittering in the distance. Lottie was very excited. "What are we going to do today?" she cried.

"Well. First things first," said Mother. "Go with the boys and get washed while I make us all some breakfast, and then we can go down to the beach."

"I can go by myself, Mother. I don't need Freddy and Ben!" shouted Lottie, running off, but a few minutes later, she reappeared, looking very sheepish. "I can't find the washroom, Mother."

"Well, you found the tent, Lottie. That's an improvement, at least," said Mother with a smile.

When the children were clean and tidy and filled with scrummy bacon sandwiches, Father gathered up the buckets and spades while Mother packed some lunch, and then they all set off to the wonderful sandy beach and blue sea for a day of adventure.

CHAPTER THREE

AN EXCITING DAY

They walked through an old
rickety gate and down a little
dusty lane. It had old stone walls, and there were
little bushes and flowers on either side, and some
prickles, too! Ben and Freddy ran ahead,
laughing and chattering, and soon disappeared
around a bend, throwing sticky bobs at each
other. Mother and Father followed with the
buckets and spades and, more
importantly, lunch for them all.

"Come along, Lottie!" Mother
shouted as Lottie dawdled
along behind. "Do keep up!"

"Look at the beautiful
butterflies!" cried Lottie,
fascinated.

Mother looked around, and could indeed see colourful butterflies flitting from bush to bush. The sun was shining and the warm air was filled with the summer sounds of buzzy bees and birdsong. "What a lovely lane this is," Mother said. "I think we should call it Butterfly Lane, Lottie."

"Oh yes, Mother. I like that name," said a beaming Lottie, jumping up and down. "Let's tell Father."

"Come along, then. Let's catch everybody up," said Mother.

As they rounded a bend in the lane, there, before them, was a magnificent sandy beach. It wasn't too big, and it wasn't too small; it was just right! It had rocks to climb on, and nooks and crannies to explore, and, best of all, small rock pools with tiny fishes and the occasional crabby crab, which the children could try and catch and put in their buckets!

"This is wonderful," said Father, spreading a blanket on the sand for them to sit on. "Now you children go and explore. Mother and I will shout you when it's time for lunch. Even you can't get lost here, Lottie!"

The sun shone, and the children laughed, and swam, or paddled, in Lottie's case, as she was just learning how to swim, and was not as confident as her brothers.

Then it was time for lunch. Mother got out packets of jam sandwiches for them all, and Father had brought a big bottle of lemonade.

After the children had eaten, sandcastles were built and knocked down, and the boys climbed on the rocks, whilst Lottie tried to catch fishes, without much success.

When it was nearly teatime, the family packed up their things and set off back down Butterfly Lane to their campsite. Lottie was very tired after all the excitement, so Father carried her on his shoulders, her hands clasped tightly around his neck, bouncing up and down as he strode along.

"Goodness," said Mother. "What a day we've had. We will all sleep like logs tonight after all this lovely fresh air and exercise. Come on everyone, let's have tea, and then it's time for bed, so we can be up bright and early for more fun tomorrow."

As the sun started to disappear, and the heat of the day faded, the little family settled into their tent for the night.

Lottie snuggled down in her sleeping bag. "I don't think I can sleep, Mother. I'm too excited!" she whispered.

"The sooner you sleep, Lottie, the sooner it's tomorrow, and we can have more adventures," said Mother. "Close your eyes now."

And eventually, the whole family went to sleep; Father gently snoring till Mother poked him in the ribs, and then all was quiet!

CHAPTER FOUR

LOTTIE GETS LOST

The moon rose in the starry night sky, and a faint curl of mist rolled in from the sea. Quiet rustlings and far away hoots could just be heard across the campsite.

Lottie's eyes opened wide, and she stayed very still in her nice, warm, cosy, sleeping bag. After a while, she wriggled a bit, and then a bit more. *Oh dear,* she thought. *I don't think I should have had that big cup of juice before bed. Now I need the toilet.* She looked over to where Mother and Father were fast asleep, and all you could see of Ben and Freddy were two mops of hair sticking out of their sleeping bags.

Lottie wriggled some more, and then some more, until she had wriggled right out of her sleeping bag. She crept to the front of the tent, and quietly unzipped the flap. A waft of cool air floated in, so Lottie hurriedly crawled out and zipped the flap back up before it woke the others. She stood up and looked around, to get her bearings. In the distance, she could see a dim yellow light glowing in the dark. *That must be the washroom,* she thought. *Brilliant! I can easily find my way there, so I won't have to bother Mother and Father. They will be pleased when they know I have managed to find the toilet on my own!*

So Lottie set off across the field towards the yellow light. The grass was damp where beads of dew had settled, and Lottie was a bit sad that she had not thought to put her rainbow wellington boots on.

Lottie ran as fast as her legs would take her. The moon, which had been shining brightly, started to disappear as the sea mist drifted across it, and the hooting and rustling fell silent.

At last, Lottie reached the washroom. She went to the toilet as quickly as she could, washed her hands in the little bowl specially for children, and then, drying them on her jammies, ran outside to get back to the tent before Father and Mother discovered she was missing. *I won't have a big cup of juice before bed again,* she thought.

As she moved away from the warm glow of the washroom light, Lottie found herself enveloped in the cold damp mist from the sea. The moon had disappeared, and as she looked around in the dark, she realised she didn't know which way to go.

I'll go back to the washroom, she thought. *I'll be safe there.* But when she turned around, all she could see was mist! *Oh no, oh no, I'm lost again,* she thought. *Mother is going to be so angry with me!*

Lottie sat down on the damp grass and started to cry. *What am I going to do? It's getting so cold!* She put her head in her hands and sobbed and sobbed.

Suddenly, out of the mist appeared a large shadow, floating towards her.

Lottie was frightened. She stopped crying, and curled up into a small ball, squeezing her eyes tightly shut, hoping the shadow wouldn't see her. But it was too late. The shadow *had* seen her, and to Lottie's horror it landed right next to her!

"Well, well, well. What have we here?" the shadow said.

Lottie opened her eyes, and there, before her, stood a huge, magnificent owl, his dark amber eyes staring at her above a large, hooked beak.

Lottie's mouth fell open in amazement and fright. "You're an owl," she squeaked.

"How very perceptive of you, young lady," the owl said in his rich, deep voice.

"But owls don't talk," said Lottie. "Perhaps I'm dreaming."

"I can assure you, you are not dreaming," said the owl. "I am very real, and I can only talk to very special children."

"But I'm not special," said Lottie. "I'm always being told off by Mother and Father for getting lost. I'm lost *now*!"

"You *must* be special," said the owl, "otherwise I couldn't talk to you. And as for being lost… well, we can soon put that right. But it's been a long, long time since I've talked to anyone, and you seem a very nice, polite young lady. Do you have a name?"

The owl's dark eyes peered deeply into Lottie's, and she found herself saying, "It's Lottie."

"What a pretty name," said the owl.

"My family call me Lottie Lostalot, because I'm always getting lost… and now I've done it again!" wailed Lottie.

The owl cocked his head to one side and blinked. He stared at Lottie, and Lottie stared back at him. Eventually, she mustered all the courage she had and, holding her head up high, asked, "Do you have a name?"

The owl stared and stared. "Mowk," he said eventually. "It's Mowk."

"Mowk," said Lottie. "That's a strange name, but I like it. I like it a lot."

The owl puffed up his feathers and blinked. "Why thank you, Lottie Lostalot. That's very kind of you."

Lottie gave a tentative smile. "It's been nice talking to you, Mowk, but I'm still lost. Do you think you can help?"

"I most certainly can," said Mowk, "but perhaps we should have a little adventure first."

CHAPTER FIVE

LOTTIE AND MOWK

Lottie looked up at Mowk, eyes still watery from sobbing. "But my family will wonder where I am if they wake up and I'm not there," she said worriedly, thinking, *this must be a dream… I can't really be talking to an owl!*

"You don't need to worry," said Mowk. "I've told you: you are a very special little girl. You have magic in you. When you are with me, time stands still. Your family will never know you've been gone. Now, how would you like to fly with me, and see the stars and the moon?"

Lottie had to admit… that sounded an amazing adventure. She would be able to tell her brothers all about it! Although, she was not so sure they would believe her.

Mowk's dark amber eyes seemed to glow in the dark as they stared, unblinkingly, into hers. Lottie found herself nodding her head in assent. "All right, then. Just a little adventure," she whispered, with a mixture of excitement and fright!

The mist swirled around as the darkness enveloped them.

"Climb up onto my back," said Mowk, "and put your arms around me."

Lottie did as she was told. Mowk's feathers were so velvety; it was like climbing into a big, soft bed. Lottie clasped her arms around him and squeaked, "I'm ready!"

Mowk spread his huge wings and, with a hop and a skip, launched himself into the air!

Lottie shut her eyes tightly, not daring to look. *This can't be happening*, she thought. *I only get lost – I don't go on adventures!*

The owl soared up into the cool night air, with Lottie clinging on for dear life, her hair streaming behind her. She looked down, but it was hard to see anything, because the mist was so thick.

As they got higher and higher, the mist got thinner and thinner, and then, all of a sudden, as Lottie looked up, she could see the stars and the moon, shining brightly in the night sky. *Oh my goodness,* she thought. *That is so beautiful.* The stars were twinkling, and the moon was so close, she was sure that if she reached out, she could touch it!

"Mowk. This is more amazing than I could ever have imagined!" shouted Lottie. "What an adventure you have brought me on!"

"I knew you would like it, Lottie," said Mowk. "As soon as I saw you, I knew you were a very special little girl."

The pair flew higher and higher, with Lottie squealing in delight as they sailed across the night sky.

Eventually, it was time for Lottie to go back to the campsite. Mowk had begun to fly lower, when suddenly; he turned his head as if listening, then let out a piercing cry.

Lottie nearly fell off his back, but managed to cling on tightly. "What is it?" she shouted, frightened. "What's the matter?"

"I have to go and meet with the Owl Council at once!" he cried. "Something terrible has happened. I can't take you back now, Lottie. You will have to come with me. But don't worry. Time is standing still for your family, so they won't miss you."

Oh dear, thought Lottie. *This is turning out to be a bigger adventure than I expected.* She was beginning to like Mowk, and wondered what the terrible thing could be. All thoughts of her family were completely gone from her mind as the pair glided across the land; a silent shadow in the moonlight.

Over hills and valleys they went, Lottie looking down as towns and villages sped past. Eventually, in the distance, a dark forest came into view. Speeding between the trees, Mowk let out a cry, and immediately, from either side, two smaller owls joined them.

They were deep in the forest now, and then, just ahead, Lottie saw a ring of trees, whose lower branches were filled with owls of all shapes and sizes... although none were as magnificent as Mowk.

They landed softly on a bed of leaves, and Lottie slid to the ground from Mowk's back. Much to her astonishment, she realized she could understand what the owls were talking about! They were very agitated, hopping up and down, making the branches bend alarmingly.

"Settle down, settle down, everybody!" shouted Mowk. "One of you step forward and tell me what has happened."

The owls looked at each other, and then one flew down and stood next to Mowk. His amber eyes stared into Mowk's as he told the sorry tale.

They had been out hunting with Kahrn, Prince of Owls. In the undergrowth, they had seen a small animal moving, and Kahrn had flown down to grab it in his claws. The animal was a small rat, and as Kahrn had swooped in, other rats had scuttled out from under leaves and branches and swarmed all over him; too fast for Kahrn to escape. They had dragged him down a large, dark tunnel into the Underworld of Rheena, Queen of Rats.

Lottie was horrified. Her eyes filled with tears. *Oh no*, she thought. *The poor owl. Such a beautiful creature. I must do all I can to help Mowk and the Owl Council rescue Kahrn!*

Everyone looked to Mowk to see what could be done. Mowk looked solemnly at them all, his eyes ablaze with anger and despair. "This is terrible news," he said. "The Rat Queen has been trying to capture our Prince for many years now. How could we have let this happen?"

CHAPTER SIX

THE DILEMMA

Mowk blinked and blinked. "Right," he said, looking at the circle of owls that surrounded him. "One of you will have to show me where Prince Kahrn was captured. We will have to go down into the Underworld to get our Prince back."

The owls looked at each other.

"Who will be brave enough to come with me?" asked Mowk.

The owls had fallen silent. The only sound was the sigh of the wind and rustle of the leaves in the treetops. No one wanted to go. Catching a rat on its own was one thing, but going down into their world… well, that was too much for the owls, and they sat on their branches with wide eyes and bowed heads!

"I'll come with you, Mowk," cried Lottie. "I want to help you rescue your Prince."

The other owls looked at Lottie, and then one of them hopped forward. "I'll come," he said in a gruff voice. "I know where the entrance to their Underworld is."

"Bravo," said Mowk, "that's the spirit. You are a very brave owl. What is your name?"

"Cosmo," answered the owl. He was not as big as Mowk, but just as splendid, with yellow eyes and tufty ears, and he looked very fierce.

Lottie climbed onto Mowk's back, and the two owls flew through the forest, gliding silently between the trees, until they came to the place where Prince Kahrn had been captured. Landing on a sturdy branch high in the treetops, Cosmo pointed a wing at a large hole in the ground; the entrance to the rats' Underworld.

Oh dear, thought Lottie, who had got off Mowk, and was now sitting on the branch. *Perhaps I was a bit hasty in saying I would help. This looks very scary indeed, and I don't like rats. They have long, skinny tails, and squeak a lot!*

Cosmo, Mowk, and Lottie sat in silence. How to rescue their Prince? That was the question.

They sat and thought, and thought and sat, and time ticked by.

"I need a plan," said Mowk. "We can't go into the Underworld, because we can't fly down there, and the rats will catch us as well. This is very tricky. Very tricky indeed…"

"I could try and go down," said Lottie, "but I think I'm too big, and I wouldn't be able to see in the dark."

The three sat in quiet despair, knowing that every minute counted if they wanted to get Prince Kahrn back alive.

"How big is the Underworld?" asked Lottie. "Is there another way in?"

"It goes all the way up to the river," said Mowk. "I'm sure there is an entrance by the riverbank."

"Can we go and see if we can find it?" asked Lottie, jumping back onto Mowk. "It might be an easier way in."

So the two owls leapt into the air, with Mowk nearly losing Lottie in the process.

Lottie squealed and held on as tight as she could as they soared into the sky, skimming the treetops. It was a full moon that cast its shadow on the forest below, and in its light, Lottie could see a ribbon of sparkle marking the course of the river.

"I see the river, I see the river!" she cried.

The owls dived down, following the river for a short while, and then landed on a very large rock next to the riverbank.

"I think the Underworld entrance is near here," said Cosmo.

"You're right," said Mowk. "I think I see it hidden in the reeds. I don't think it will help us, though. It's still too small for Lottie."

The two owls were very upset, and Lottie didn't know what to do. She liked Mowk a lot, and really wanted to help him and all the other owls in the forest. She gave a big sigh, and thought till her head hurt.

"I think I may have an idea," she said eventually, "but we may need help."

CHAPTER SEVEN

LOTTIE'S IDEA

"What is your idea, Lottie?" asked Mowk.

"Well," said Lottie. "I think it's rather brilliant, actually. If we can't go down into the Underworld to get Prince Kahrn, then he will have to come to us!"

"Oh my goodness, Lottie! Whatever do you mean? How can Prince Kahrn come to us? He can't fly in the Underworld, and the rats have him trapped!" cried Mowk.

"It's simple," Lottie said with a smile. "We can direct some of the river into the Underworld entrance, and it will wash him out the other end, along with all the rats!"

Cosmo and Mowk looked at Lottie in amazement.

"You know, Lottie… that might just work. That is a brilliant idea," said Mowk. "But you're right: we are going to need help. Cosmo, go and get the rest of the Owl Council, and all the owls in the forest. We need to build a dam so part of the river flows down into the Underworld. Lottie and I will get started. Hurry now, Cosmo. Fly like the wind!"

It wasn't long before owls started to arrive from all over the forest. They carried branches in their talons, and twigs in their beaks, and soon a dam began to take shape.

When Cosmo returned, Mowk put him in charge of the dam building. "Lottie and I will go to the other entrance now. Let us know when you are ready to let the water into the Underworld, and when the rats are washed out, along with Prince Kahrn, we will be able to rescue him!"

Lottie climbed back onto Mowk's back, and off they went, swooping between the trees, up and down and side to side. They flew so close to the branches that Lottie could almost reach out and grab their leaves. Her hair streamed behind her and her cheeks were red from the touch of the cool night air.

When they arrived at the other entrance to the Underworld, Mowk landed gently on the ground and Lottie slid off his back, ruffling some feathers as she went. Thankfully, there was no sign of the rats, so Lottie crawled as close to the entrance as she could.

"I think I'm ready now," she whispered to Mowk. "When the water comes rushing out, I will try and catch Prince Kahrn before the rats realize I'm here." Her eyes were wide, and she was very nervous. It was her plan, after all, and she was not entirely sure it would work.

Mowk flew to the top of the tree and perched on the highest branch, waiting for the signal from Cosmo to say they were ready to let the river flood into the Underworld. It was hard work for the owls, collecting all the wood required for the job, but not one of them complained. They would do anything to save their Prince.

It was very dark on the forest floor, so Lottie crawled a bit nearer to the Underworld entrance, being as quiet as she could be. She looked up at the sky, and in the light of the moon, could see the outline of Mowk sitting on his branch, waiting for Cosmo's signal to say all was ready. Little noises from the forest floor made her jump, and she had to be stern with herself. *Come on, Lottie. You can do this. What are you, man, or mouse?* That's what Father would say.

Lottie blinked a few times, and took a deep breath. Then she heard Mowk shout, "The water is coming, Lottie! Be ready!"

At first, Lottie couldn't hear anything. Then she felt the ground shiver beneath her, and suddenly a huge spout of water gushed out of the entrance. Lottie jumped back, startled, not realizing it would be so fierce, and then rats came tumbling out, squeaking and gasping for air.

Straining her eyes, Lottie could just make out the shape of something a lot larger, and moving closer, she realized it was Kahrn, Prince of Owls.

She plunged into the rushing sea of water and rats and grabbed hold of Prince Kahrn, dragging him as best she could out on to a dry part of the forest floor. Then Mowk swooped down, picked up the bedraggled owl in his talons, and carried him gently into the treetops.

The rats were swept away by the water, which Lottie was very thankful for, and suddenly Mowk was there beside her. "Come on Lottie, climb on quickly. We must get out of here before the rats can gather themselves and come back."

Lottie flung herself onto Mowk's back and sank into his soft downy feathers.

They flew back to where the Owl Council met.

Once Mowk had settled on his perch, he called the council to order. "Settle down, everyone. Settle down. It is thanks to Lottie that our great

Prince has been rescued. We cannot tell you, Lottie, how grateful we are for your magnificent plan, and your bravery in carrying it out. Our Prince wants you to accept our eternal thanks, and to know that we will always be at your service. If you are ever in trouble, we will know about it and be there by your side."

Lottie was a little overwhelmed, and could only just get her words out.

"Thank you all," she whispered. "I am so glad that I could help. Who knew that getting lost would take me on such an amazing adventure?"

CHAPTER EIGHT

A DREAM OR NOT A DREAM

Now that all the excitement was over, Lottie suddenly felt very, *very* tired. She snuggled in amongst Mowk's feathers and fell into a deep sleep.

When she woke up, Lottie found herself back in her tent, in her sleeping bag. The family was just starting to stir; the two boys play fighting with their pillows.

"Now now, boys!" cried Mother. "Stop that at once. The tent is much too small for such things. Get your wash bags and go and have a good shower. You too, Lottie. There is no place for sleepyheads in this tent. We have lots of adventures to go on."

Lottie smiled to herself. *If only they knew*, she thought. *I've already been on the best adventure of my life… unless it was all just a dream. Oh, I do hope it wasn't a dream!* But the harder she tried to remember what had happened, the more she convinced herself it was just a dream, after all.

"Wait for me!" she cried as the boys ran off down the field. "I don't want to get lost!"

As Lottie wriggled out of her sleeping bag, she could feel something in the pocket of her jammies. Putting her hand in, she pulled out a magnificent feather, and heard a voice whisper in her ear: "We will always be here for you, Lottie. You saved our Prince, and we will never forget!"

THE END

If you would like to know more about the Author or Illustrator, and other books they have written, then you can visit the Authors website at

pjsandz.com

And the Illustrators social media

@WeAreAlienBand